Cooper's Tale

By Ralph da Costa Nunez

with Willow Schrager

Illustrated by Madeline Gerstein Simon

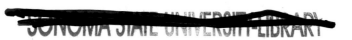

Published in the United States by
Institute for Children and Poverty, Inc.
36 Cooper Square, 6th Floor
New York, New York 10003
(212) 529-5252

Printed in the United States of America

Introduction

Fifteen years ago I met my first homeless family. But of all that I've learned during that time, what remains most shocking to me—and most overlooked by others—is the fact that so many of the homeless in America are children. Although you don't often see homeless families on the streets, because they live in emergency shelters or doubled and tripled up with other families, they are there: they are in fact the hidden homeless, and most are young children.

One of the most tragic parts of homeless children's lives is their loss of education. Many repeat grades in school, some never learn to read, and others drop out, all because they had no quiet place to study, no stable place to stay, and no place to call home.

As you read Cooper's Tale, remember how easy it can be for someone to lose his home and become homeless, and imagine how devastating and traumatic that can be for a child.

Today, homelessness is no longer simply about housing. Today it is about education, about families, and more than ever, about children. Cooper's Tale is more than just a story of a mouse and how he loses his home; it reflects the stories of more than one million homeless children across America. Just like Cooper, their stories need a happy ending too, and working together we can make that happen.

Leonard N. Stern
Founder/Chairman
Homes for the Homeless
New York City

Once there was a pink mouse named Cooper who lived and worked in a cheese shop. The old man who owned the cheese shop liked Cooper very much because he would always help the man clean up by eating all the crumbs on the floor.

Cooper liked the old man because he would always drop a few extra crumbs for Cooper to eat, and would pretend that it was an accident. The mouse and the man were happy together living in the little shop.

One lazy morning Cooper woke up to the sun shining into his mouse hole. He yawned, stretched, and got ready to keep the old man company while mousing about the shop. But when Cooper came out of his hole, he could tell that something was wrong. The shop was quiet and still. Cooper looked around. He couldn't see the old man anywhere.

"Squeak Squeak," Cooper called out, but the old man didn't answer. Confused, Cooper tip-toed a couple of laps around the cheese shop, then returned to his hole. He stayed there all that day and part of the next, waiting for the old man to return. He was lonely without his friend.

Finally on the second day, Cooper heard the shop door open and someone come in. He jumped up excitedly and ran out to greet the old man. But Cooper screeched to a stop in the middle of the room and looked up, surprised.

The old man was not there. Instead, towering over him was a lady in a big red hat.
At her side were the two biggest, fattest cats Cooper had ever seen.

The woman reached down and picked Cooper up by his tail. Cooper squirmed in mid-air. The woman laughed out loud and said to her two cats, "Boris, Frank, look at this silly creature. Who ever heard of a *pink* mouse?"

Then the woman held Cooper close to her face and yelled, "I am the new owner of this cheese shop. You have to pay to live here now. The fat cats are in town!" She, Boris, and Frank all burst out laughing. The woman dropped Cooper to the floor.

Cooper knew that he had no money to pay the woman, and that he would have to leave his home. As he sat on the edge of his bed, a mouse tear slid down his pink cheek.

His whiskers quivered with sadness. He missed the old man. "Where will I go now?" he thought to himself, "What will happen to me?"

Cooper began packing his few belongings into a small suitcase—a ball of string, his favorite green yo-yo, a broken mirror, two rubber bands, and three large crumbs of cheese that he had been saving for a special day. He waited until everything was quiet. Then he snuck out of the cheese shop.

He wandered the streets for several hours with his mousecase, wondering what to do next. He felt lost and alone and scared. Where would he sleep tonight? Where would he find crumbs to eat?

It began to get cold. Cooper's small feet hurt, and his mousecase was beginning to feel very heavy. He had to find somewhere to go, and soon. Just then, he looked up and noticed that he was standing in front of a school playground. There were lots and lots of children running around, laughing, and playing games.

Cooper wondered if they could help him. He watched for quite a while, trying to figure out how to get their attention without scaring them…and without getting stepped on.

Then he noticed two boys and a little girl who were not playing. They were sitting quietly against the fence, watching the other kids. Cooper crept out from his hiding place and bravely approached them. But once he was standing in front of them, Cooper was suddenly shy. He didn't know what to say, so he just said "Hello" quietly, and waited.

The little girl looked down at him and tilted her head curiously. "Hi," she replied. Cooper blushed, which made him even more pink than he already was. But he found enough courage to squeak, "Why aren't you playing with the other kids?"

The oldest boy said sadly, "We're different. We're not like most kids– we're homeless." The little girl shook her pigtails and said, "We don't feel different. But here at school they say we are." Cooper thought for a moment and then asked, "Homeless? What does that mean?" "It means that we don't have a place to live," said the girl.

"Oh," said Cooper, "Then I think I might be homeless, too. You see, I used to live and work in a cheese shop. I lived with an old man who was my friend. But the fat cats came and wanted me to pay a lot of rent, so I had to leave."

"We know how you feel," the younger boy said. "My name is James. Our mom worked too, but then our rent went up and we couldn't pay it either. Hey, maybe the fat cats who raised your rent were the ones who raised our rent too! After that, we had to go live in a homeless shelter."

"What's a shelter?" asked Cooper. James smiled and said, "That's a place where homeless people can go and have a place to sleep and food to eat. This is my brother, Michael, and my sister, Maria. We all live in the homeless shelter. That's why people think we're different from the other kids."

"Well then I guess I'm different, too," said Cooper in a sad mouse whisper. "Because you're pink?" asked Maria. Cooper looked down at himself sheepishly and blushed. "No…I never let that bother me very much. But now," he said with a mouse sniffle, "now I'm homeless too." Maria felt so sad for him. She thought that he was about to cry.

Suddenly her eyes lit up. "I have an idea!" she said. "Why don't you come back to the shelter with us?" Cooper turned a bright shade of pink and said that he would love to. He felt so happy that he actually hugged her ankle. Everyone laughed, including Cooper.

It was time for Michael, James, and Maria to go inside again. Cooper promised that he would meet them after school. He tried to pass the time by pretending that he was a great warrior-mouse, battling the empty-soda-can monster. When he was tired of that, he followed a large black beetle around in circles until he was dizzy.

Finally, Cooper heard the school bell ring. The children came rushing out. Michael and James and Maria ran over to him. "Ready to go?" they asked. Cooper grinned and nodded. Maria picked him up gently and placed him and his mousecase into the pocket of her shirt. Cooper poked his head out of the top of her pocket. He had a perfect view.

When they arrived at the shelter, the children showed Cooper around and introduced him to a few of their friends. There were lots of children living at the shelter. Then Michael, James, and Maria took Cooper to their room and made him a little space of his own in the corner.

They even gave him a sock to sleep in.

Cooper was comfortable in his new bed. He was happy with his new friends, but he missed the old man. That night Cooper fell asleep wondering if he would ever see him again.

When Cooper woke up the next morning, the children were at breakfast with their mother. Cooper yawned, stretched, and wiggled his way out of his sock. He went into the shelter's library, pulled a book off the shelf, and began to read.

When the children came back from breakfast, they found Cooper in the library. "What are you doing?" they asked. "Reading a story," answered Cooper. Maria opened her eyes wide and said, "Oh…we don't know how to read." Cooper looked surprised. "Why not?" he asked.

"Well," Maria explained, "Because when you're homeless you don't live in the same place very long, and so you are not in the same school very long. So it was hard for us to keep up with our school work. We fell behind."

Cooper stood up as tall as he could and put on his most serious face. "Then I will teach you how to read," said Cooper, "because you all taught me about homelessness. We can learn from each other. Reading is fun–you'll see."

"Fun?" asked James. "Really?" "Oh yes!" squeaked Cooper. "And it's very important to know how to read. If you know how to read then you can do well in school. And if you do well in school then you can be anything you want."

"What do you want to be when you grow up?" he asked the children. "I want to be a doctor," said James. "I want to be an astronaut," said Michael. "I want to be a police officer," said Maria. "Good," said Cooper, "then let's try to read together."

Maria picked up the book and sat down on the floor with her two brothers. Cooper perched on top of the open book with his tail hanging over the edge and began showing the children how to sound out the words. He walked excitedly back and forth across the top of the book. Michael, James, and Maria took turns trying to read each line.

The other children who were playing in the room stopped and came over to listen. "Can we read too?" they asked. "Of course!" smiled Cooper. "We all can learn to read together."

Every night after that,   Cooper, Michael, James

and Maria read together   before they went to bed.

Sometimes Cooper would read out loud to them, and once the

children got good enough, they would read to him. It was always

a very special time for them to spend together.

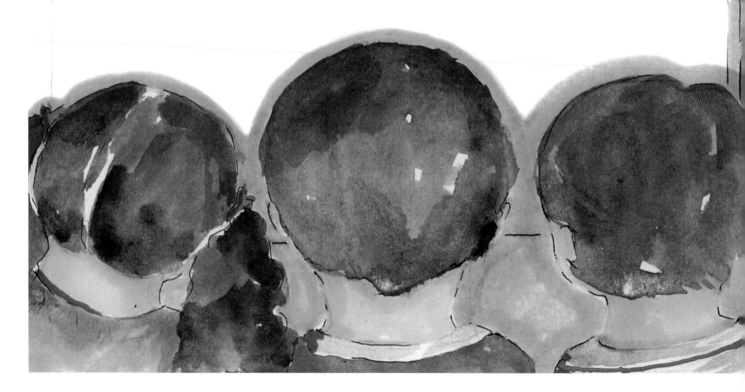

One morning many months later, the children were late for school.
One,

    two,

        three, they kissed their mother good-bye and rushed out the door. Because they were late, they decided to take a short-cut through the park. As usual, Cooper was bouncing along in Maria's pocket with only his nose and whiskers poking out. Suddenly he let out a loud squeak. "Wait, STOP!" he called out. The three children stopped so quickly that bump,

                bump,

                    bump, they ran right into each other.

Cooper climbed out of Maria's pocket and scampered over to an old man sitting on a bench feeding the birds. Cooper ran right up his leg, climbed onto his shoulder, and gave him a big hug (well, as big as a *mouse* hug can be).

The old man was smiling from ear to ear. "Hello my little pink friend!" he said warmly. Surprised, Michael, James, and Maria just stood and stared. "It's my friend, the cheese shop man," Cooper shouted. He was so happy that he could barely squeak out the words.

"What happened to you?" Cooper asked. "I missed you so much." "I missed you too," said the man. "I got very sick and had to go to the hospital."

"Who are your new friends?" he asked. "Oh, of course," said Cooper. "This is Michael, this is James, and this is Maria. They took me to live with them at the homeless shelter."

"Why are you children homeless?" the man asked. "Our rent went up, so we had to leave our home," said Michael. "That's terrible," said the man. Then he thought for a moment. "Hmmm...I just might be able to help you. After all, friends of Cooper's are friends of mine!" he said with a wink.

The children all looked at each other and wondered what he had in mind. "You kids should go to school now, or you'll be late. Cooper, you come with me," said the old man.

That day when the children returned from school, the old man was waiting at the homeless shelter with their mother and Cooper. All three were smiling big smiles. "We have a surprise for you," they said.

"Remember the story I told you about why I had to leave the cheese shop?" Cooper asked the children. Michael, James, and Maria nodded. "Well, the old man made the lady and her fat cats leave. But he is living with his daughter now, and there is no one to run the shop. So we were thinking…"

"How would you kids like to live in the apartment above the cheese shop, and your mom and Cooper can run the shop for me?" asked the old man. "It's very close to your school, and near the park." The three children all ran over and hugged the man and hugged their mother.

"Oh, our own home! It will be perfect!" shouted James, jumping up and down.
"And we'll be able to continue our reading lessons," Cooper squeaked. All the
children cheered. Maria scooped up Cooper and gave him a big kiss on his pink
cheek. Cooper blushed.

That day, Cooper packed up his mousecase and went home to the cheese shop with the children and their mother. When he got there he was so excited that he ran into his hole and hugged his bed.

Then he opened his mousecase and took out his ball of string. He put his favorite green yo-yo back on the shelf. He hung his broken mirror on the wall again. He put his two rubber bands back in their hiding place under the bed. And he put his favorite book under his pillow, just like before. Very soon everything felt normal again.

That night, Cooper tucked himself into his warm, cozy bed. He fell asleep smiling and thinking about what he would do the next day, the first day of his new life.

Tonight over one million
*child*ren
will be homeless in America.

For more information about family homelessness and what you can do to help, contact Homes
for the Homeless at (212) 529-5252 or visit www.homesforthehomeless.com